This igloo book belongs to:

....

igloobooks

Published in 2019
by Igloo Books Ltd
Cottage Farm
Sywell
NN6 0BJ
www.igloobooks.com

1219 001
2 4 6 8 10 9 7 5 3 1
ISBN 978-1-83903-303-2

Original story by Anna Sewell
Retold by Melanie Joyce
Illustrated by Diane Le Feyer

Designed by Justine Ablett
Edited by Stephanie Moss

Printed and manufactured in China

Black
Beauty
igloobooks

My early home was a pleasant meadow, where I lived with my mother, Duchess. **"You are well bred,"** she said. **"I want you to grow to be gentle and not kick or bite."** I never forgot my mother's advice, for she was a wise old horse.

Time passed in that happy place and I grew to be handsome. My coat was glossy black, with one white foot and a pretty white star on my forehead. Then, when I was four years old, my master taught me to wear a saddle and bridle, as well as pull a carriage. I learnt to always obey my master's will, without the freedom of my early life.

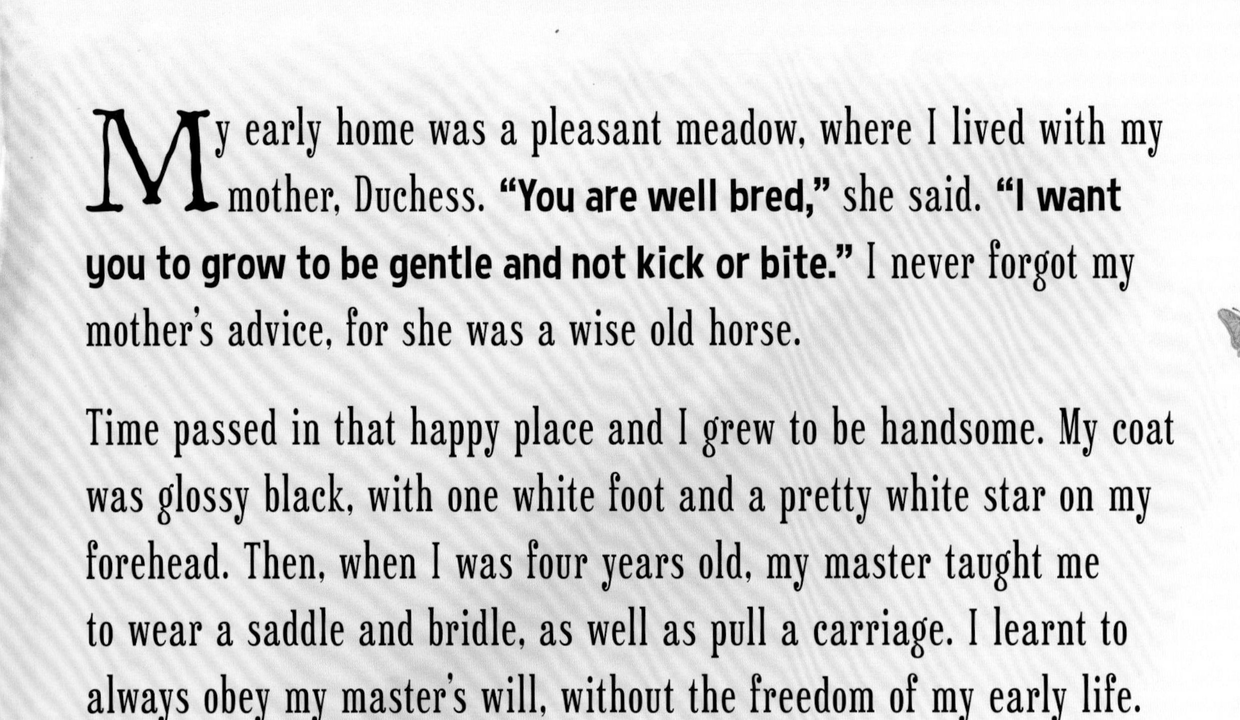

My training was soon complete, and early that May I was bought by a Squire Gordon and taken to Birtwick Park. At the stables, I was put in a comfortable stall that was clean and airy. Next to me was a fat, grey pony called Merrylegs, who thought himself very handsome indeed.

Across the way was a chestnut mare, looking over from her stall.
Like me, she was about fifteen hands high, but she seemed bad-tempered.
"That's Ginger," said Merrylegs. **"People have been unkind to her, so she snaps and bites sometimes, even though our grooms, John and James, are very kind."**

I soon settled into my new home. Squire Gordon named me Black Beauty and put me in the carriage with Ginger, who told me how she had been cruelly treated. With time, Ginger grew much less cross. She and Merrylegs became my dearest friends.

One day, my master went to town for business and I was stabled there for the night with Ginger. As John settled us down, I noticed a man with a pipe come in.

I thought nothing of it until later, when I saw a red light and a thick, grey cloud across the stalls.

Someone shouted, **"Fire!"** But John spoke gently to me and led me outside.

I whinnied because I could not see Ginger, but at last James brought her out, too. She said that if I had not called to her, she would not have had the courage to move.

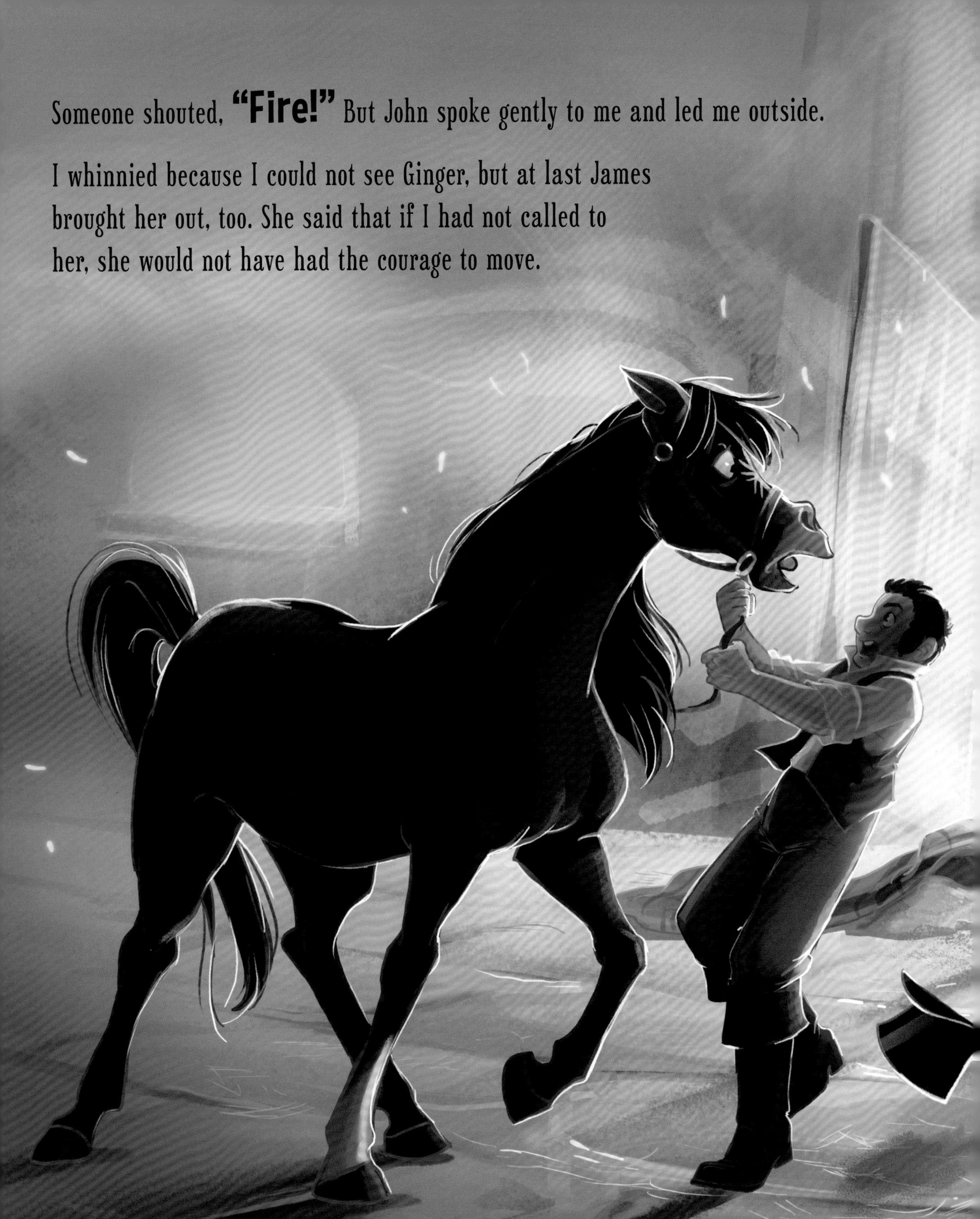

Soon after that terrible night, James left and a new groom, Joe Green, arrived. He was kind, but inexperienced.

One night, the mistress fell ill and I raced to the doctor's house. I was hot from galloping, so Joe did not put my rug on and I caught a terrible chill.

John looked after me and I soon became well again, but it was not the same for my mistress. Her health was poor, and soon she and the master moved to a warmer climate. Ginger and I were sold to an Earl, and Merrylegs was given to a vicar. I held my face close to John's, as that was all I could do to say goodbye.

Our new home at Earlshall was not as pleasant as Birtwick. Ginger and I had to wear uncomfortable bearing reins, and we missed Merrylegs. One night when the master was away, the groom, Reuben Smith, rode me home from town, drunk. There were sharp stones on the road and I lost a shoe, but he forced me to gallop.

I went at such a speed, I stumbled and fell on my knees. I quickly got up, but Reuben was lying on the ground. He groaned, then lay still, for he was dead.

Everyone knew I was not to blame, but my knees were damaged and I needed a long rest.

I was put into a paddock by myself and felt very lonely, until one day, Ginger arrived. I was so happy to see her and to have that time together.

But it was not long after that I was taken away and sold, with only a sad whinny of goodbye to my dear old friend.

In my time after Earlshall, I became a job horse and was let out to anyone that wished to hire me. There were many bad drivers, but some good ones, too. Because I was patient and good-natured, one such driver recommended me to a man called Mr Barry, who became my new owner.

My master knew little about horses but treated me well. I would have had an easy time of it, had it not been for one groom who stole my feeding oats, and another, Alfred Smirk, who did not clean my stable properly.

My feet became tender and sore, and I was soon lame.

Mr Barry discovered the truth, and made sure I was fed and cared for. But he was so annoyed at being deceived by the two grooms, he decided not to keep a horse any longer. When my feet were better, I was sold again, this time to a cab driver called Jeremiah Barker.

Jerry, as Jeremiah was known, was a good master and I had never known a family as happy as his. Polly, Jerry's wife, his daughter Dolly and son Harry petted and fussed me. I was stabled with their old white horse, Captain, and we were well looked after.

What a team Jerry and I made, trotting past traffic, through the streets of London. The days were long, but I was happy in my work. Then, one winter, after nights spent waiting in the cold, Jerry fell ill. He was no longer able to work and, sadly, sent me to be sold.

My life as a cab horse after that was very hard indeed. I was so overworked that I became exhausted and ended up at a horse fair. I was bought by a kind man called Farmer Thoroughgood. He said that with rest and care I would soon recover.

After a winter of good food and a comfortable stable, I was like my old self again. One sunny day, I was groomed until my coat shone.

My mane was combed and my hooves were painted.

Farmer Thoroughgood explained that he had found the perfect home for me, and I was taken to a pretty house, where three ladies lived.

Miss Blomefield, Miss Ellen and Miss Lavinia were my new owners, and liked me very much. A groom came to feed me and noticed the white star on my forehead and my one white foot.

"Why, it's Black Beauty!"
he cried, for it was Joe Green.

Joe was the best and kindest of grooms, and the ladies promised I would never be sold. I had nothing to fear and, at last, all my troubles were over.

Sometimes, however, I would wake at night and imagine I was still in the orchard at Birtwick Park, standing with my old friends under the apple tree.